THE USBORNE BOOK OF
BODY
FACTS

Anita Ganeri

KT-574-928

CONTENTS

Illustrated by Allan Robinson and Guy Smith

Designed by Allan Robinson

Consultant: Professor T. G. Baker D.Sc., F.R.C.Path., F.R.S.E.

With thanks to Dr Ann Woodford M.B., Ch.B.

Your body

Who am I?

All living things are made up of tiny units, called cells. Your body is made of about 50 million million cells. Some make up your skin, bones and other body parts. Some convert food and oxygen into energy to keep you going. Others carry messages around your body or fight off germs. Cells come in different shapes and sizes, depending on the job they do.

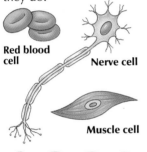

Red blood cell

Nerve cell

Muscle cell

The main parts of a cell

1. Cell membrane
2. Cytoplasm
3. Nucleus
4. Mitochondria
5. Endoplasmic reticulum
6. Golgi tubes
7. Lysosomes

1. Cell membrane The cell's very thin, outer "skin". It lets food and oxygen into the cell and lets waste products out of the cell.

2. Cytoplasm A jelly-like substance which makes up most of the cell. Other parts of the cell float in it.

3. Nucleus The cell's control unit. It carries instructions, called genes, which tell the cell how to work and keep it alive.

4. Mitochondria The cell's power stations. They use oxygen to release energy from food.

5. Endoplasmic reticulum The cell's proteins are made here. Proteins are used for growth and repair.

6. Golgi tubes Storage areas for proteins until the cell needs them.

7. Lysosomes Containers for chemicals which destroy old or diseased cell parts and keep out harmful substances.

DID YOU KNOW?

Most cells are too small to see except under a microscope. Female egg cells (ova) are the biggest cells. Each is about the size of the dot over this letter " i ". The smallest cells are in your brain. They are 100 times smaller than ova.

Tissue types

Your body tissues include skin, muscle, blood, nerve and bone tissue. Tissues are groups of cells working together. They may be cells of the same type or cells of different types. The tiny spaces between the cells are filled with a watery liquid which is called interstitial fluid.

Body organs

Organs are groups of tissues which work together. They include your heart and lungs. The liver is the biggest organ. In adults, it weighs over 1.5kg (3.3lb), as much as six medium oranges. Groups of organs working together form systems, such as your digestive system.

Cell lifespans

Some of your cells last a lifetime. Others are constantly being replaced and renewed. Here you can see how long some cells live.

Type of cell	Average lifespan
Cells lining small intestine	2-3 days
Taste bud cells	7 days
Skin cells	3 weeks
Red blood cells	4 months
Bone cells	25-30 years
Muscle cells	Most last a lifetime
Nerve and brain cells	Some last a lifetime

Splitting up

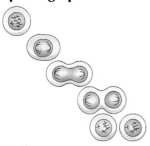

Until you are 18-20 years old, new cells are constantly being made to make you grow. Most cells reproduce by splitting in two. A cell gets larger, then divides to form a pair of identical new cells. Cells also divide to replace dead or worn out cells.

Cell science

No one knew that cells existed until 1665. Then an English scientist, called Robert Hooke, discovered tiny units in a piece of cork he was examining under a home-made microscope. The idea that all living things are made of cells was first suggested in 1839.

Amazing But True

By weight, your cells, and therefore your whole body, are almost two-thirds water. This means that you contain enough water to fill about 1½ large buckets.

Warm-blooded

Human beings are warm-blooded. This means that the temperature inside our bodies stays much the same all the time. Normal body temperature is 37°C (98.6°F). This is the temperature at which our cells work best. Warm clothes, cool drinks, sweating and shivering help keep it stable.

Highs and lows

If your body temperature rises or falls by just a few degrees, it can be very dangerous. You can die if it falls below 25°C (77°F) or if it rises above 41°C (106°F).

Body framework

Skeleton scaffold

Without a skeleton, your body would collapse in a heap. Your skeleton holds your body up and gives it shape. It provides firm anchorage for your muscles so you can move. It also protects delicate organs, such as your heart, lungs, brain and spinal cord.

How many bones?

Most adults have 206 separate bones in their skeletons. A newborn baby has over 300 bones, but some of them join, or fuse, together as it gets older. Over half your bones are found in your hands and feet. There are 26 bones in each foot and 27 in each hand. These bones allow you to make very small, precise movements.

What's in a bone?

Hard outside
Spongy inside

Marrow

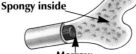

A bone is a living structure made up of water, minerals such as calcium, and a tough protein, collagen. The outer part is very hard, but the inside is softer and spongy. Some bones contain a substance called marrow which makes red blood cells.

Brain box

Suture

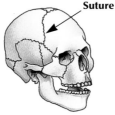

Your delicate brain is well protected inside your cranium, the main part of your skull. This "brain box" is actually eight separate bones. As you get older, the bones gradually join together to make your skull stronger. The places where the bones join are visible as wiggly lines, called sutures.

Flexible backbone

Animals which have backbones and skeletons inside their bodies are called vertebrates. Your backbone is a flexible chain of 26 bones. The topmost bone supports your skull. It is called the atlas bone after the Greek god, Atlas. In legend, he carried the world on his shoulders.

Record-breaking bones

Longest bone	Femur (thighbone)
Strongest bone	Femur (thighbone)
Smallest bone	Stapes (stirrup-shaped bone inside the ear)
Largest joint	Knee joint
Smallest joint	Between bones inside ears

Name those bones

All the bones in your body have a scientific name. Many also have a common name.

Scientific name	Common name
Cranium	Skull
Zygoma	Cheekbone
Mandible	Jawbone
Clavicle	Collarbone
Scapula	Shoulder blade
Sternum	Breastbone
Vertebrae	Backbone
Pelvis	Hips
Carpals	Wrist bones
Phalanges	Finger and toe bones
Femur	Thighbone
Patella	Kneecap
Tibia	Shinbone
Tarsals	Ankle bones

Bone brawn

Bone is one of the strongest materials. Bones are much lighter than steel or concrete, but, weight for weight, they are much stronger. A bone is five times stronger than a steel bar of the same weight. Bones make up about 14% of your body weight.

Multi-jointed

Many of your bones meet at joints. These allow you to bend and move. At a joint, the bones are held in place by strong straps, called ligaments. The ends of the bones are covered in pads of tough gristly cartilage, to prevent wear and tear. They are kept "oiled" by a special fluid, called synovial fluid. If you are "double-jointed", it just means that you have extra long ligaments in your joints and can bend them farther than usual.

Types of joints

There are about 100 joints in your body. They can be divided into five main types:

1. Hinge – knees, elbows and fingers.

2. Ball and socket – shoulders and hips.

3. Sliding – between ankles and toes.

4. Saddle – at bases of thumbs.

5. Pivot – in wrists.

DID YOU KNOW?

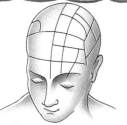

In the 19th century, some people believed that you could tell a person's character and special talents by feeling the bulges and bony lumps in their skull. This study is called phrenology. The skull is divided up into 37 areas. Each is said to represent a particular talent or characteristic.

Muscle power

Making a move

Without muscles, you would not be able to move. There are muscles all over your body, even in your heart, eyes and skin. Many muscles are attached to your bones. They pull on bones to move parts of your body, such as your arms and legs. Muscles inside your body also make you breathe and help you digest your food. These muscles work even when you are asleep.

Achilles heel

Your muscles are attached to your bones by strong bands, called tendons. The biggest tendon is the Achilles tendon in your heel. It looks and feels hard like a bone. It is named after the Greek warrior, Achilles. He died from a wound to his heel, the only part of his body that had not been dipped in the legendary river of immortality.

Team work

When you want to move a part of your body, electrical signals run from your brain along nerves to your muscles and tell them to get shorter, or contract. As they contract, they pull on parts of your body. Muscles can only pull, not push, so they often work in pairs. One muscle (the biceps) pulls to bend your elbow. Then it relaxes and its partner (the triceps) pulls to straighten your arm.

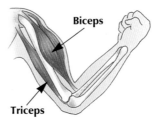

Biceps

Triceps

DID YOU KNOW?

With regular exercise and practice, you can increase the strength of your muscles. Some Olympic weightlifters are so strong they can lift three times their own weight above their heads.

Making faces

Some muscles, such as those in your face, do not move bones. They pull on your skin to change your expression. Muscles in your cheeks contract to pull up the sides of your mouth into a smile. Raising your eyebrows uses over 30 muscles.

A large bite

Your strongest muscles are the masseters on each side of your mouth. They allow you to bite into things with a force of 73kg (160lb). This is equivalent to the weight of 18 house bricks.

Taking control

Some muscles, such as those in your heart, work automatically. These are called involuntary muscles. But we can control most of our muscles, such as those in our arms and legs. These are voluntary muscles.

How much muscle?

Most people have about 640 muscles in their bodies. Muscles make up over á third of your body weight. The biggest are the gluteus maximus muscles in your buttocks and thighs. The smallest are the stapedius muscles. These muscles are attached to the tiny bones inside your ear and are less than 1.25mm (0.05in) long.

Amazing But True

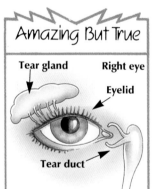

Tear gland   Right eye

Eyelid

Tear duct

The fastest-working muscles are those in your eyelids. They make you blink about 20,000 times a day. Blinking coats your eyes with tear fluid, made in your tear gland, which washes away dust and germs.

Some major muscles

Muscle	Function
Biceps	Bends elbow.
Triceps	Straightens arm.
Sartorius	Bends hip.
Gluteus maximus	Straightens hip.
Trapezius	Lifts shoulder.
Hamstring	Bends knee.
Tongue	Squeezes food and helps you swallow it.
Cardiac muscle	Makes your heart beat.

Overworked muscles

Muscles need oxygen and food for energy from your blood in order to work properly. If they work hard but do not get enough, they may go into a spasm, and you feel the pain of cramp. If you exercise soon after a meal, your muscles may cramp up because energy is being used to digest your food instead of to fuel your muscles.

The inside story

Muscles are made up of bundles of thread-like fibres. There are over 2,000 fibres inside a big muscle. The longest measure 30cm (12in). Each fibre is made up of even finer threads, called myofibrils. Muscles also contain tiny nerves and blood vessels. Covering them is a stretchy "skin", called the epimysium.

Tailor made

The sartorius is your longest muscle. It runs from your pelvis to your knee. It helps you cross your legs. It gets its name from the Latin word *sartor* meaning "tailor". In olden times, tailors often sat cross-legged to sew. The muscle with the longest name is the *levator labii superioris alaeque nasi*. It curls your lip.

Myofibrils   Epimysium

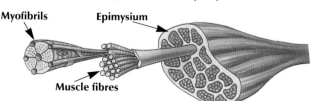

Muscle fibres

Your heart

Heavy hearted?

An adult's heart is the size of a clenched fist and weighs about 300g (10.5oz), as much as a large potato. It is divided into four chambers by walls of muscle. The two upper chambers, called the atria, are connected by tubes to the two lower chambers, called the ventricles.

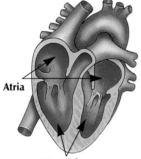

Atria

Ventricles

Blood pumping

Your heart's job is to pump blood around your body. Its muscles contract and squeeze out blood. The left-hand side of the heart pumps blood from your lungs to the rest of your body, which it supplies with oxygen. The right-hand side pumps stale blood from your body back to your lungs for a fresh supply of oxygen.

Hole in the heart

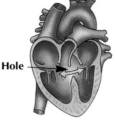

Hole

Some babies are born with a hole in the heart. This is a hole between the two atria or between the two ventricles. It allows blood from the two sides of the heart to mix so that the baby only gets a low oxygen supply going around its body. The hole has to be sewn up at an early age.

Amazing But True

At rest, each heartbeat pumps a third of a cup of blood around your body. At this rate it would take 15 minutes to fill four buckets with blood. When you exercise, it pumps out six times as much blood. The pump is so powerful that it only takes a minute for a blood cell to travel around your body and back to your heart.

Heartbeat

Your heart pumps, or beats, about once every second. This is about 100,000 times a day throughout your whole life. Each time it beats, it sends blood surging through your body. You can feel this surge as the throbbing pulse in your wrist or neck.

Nonstop working

Most of your heart is made of cardiac muscle. Unlike many of your muscles, the cardiac muscle never gets tired and never stops working until you die. It pushes blood in a continuous flow around your body. Your heart has its own blood supply, brought by the coronary arteries.

Examples of pulse rates

Your pulse rate measures how often your heart beats in one minute. It beats faster during exercise in order to supply your muscles with extra energy. An adult's heart is stronger than a child's, so it beats more slowly.

Category	Pulse rate
Average adult man (at rest)	70
Average adult woman (at rest)	80
Average adult (during exercise)	over 150
Sleeping adult	under 60
Sleeping baby	120
Ten-year-old child	100 and below
Racing car driver (during race)	200
Shrew	600
Elephant	25

DID YOU KNOW?

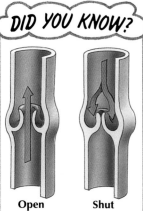

Open   **Shut**

Special valves in your heart stop your blood from flowing the wrong way through it. They are forced open by the pumped blood, then snap shut to prevent it from flowing back. As they shut they make the familiar "thump thump" sound of a heartbeat. This is the sound doctors hear when they listen to your chest with a stethoscope.

Heart under attack

In western countries, heart disease is a common cause of death. It may be caused by a blockage in the blood vessels supplying the heart muscle with oxygen and food. This stops the heart from working properly. Heart attacks can be fatal. If your heart stops beating, you die after about five minutes. Today, hospitals and ambulances have machines which can make a heart start beating again.

A healthy heart

Being under stress or overweight, eating fatty foods and smoking can all increase the risk of heart disease. Some types of heart disease are inherited. Exercising and eating a healthy diet can help reduce the danger to your heart.

A new heart

The first ever heart transplant operation was carried out in South Africa in December 1967 by the surgeon, Christian Barnard, and a team of 30 helpers. The patient only lived for 18 days. Today, heart transplant patients live for many years with their new hearts.

Life blood

Blood functions

An average adult has about 5 litres (8.7 pints) of blood. Its main functions are:

To carry oxygen from the lungs all over the body.
To collect carbon dioxide and other wastes from the cells for disposal.
To carry water and nutrients around the body.
To carry special body chemicals, called hormones.
To fight infection through the white blood cells.
To keep the body at a steady temperature.

Circulatory system

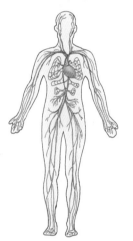

Blood flows from your heart along strong tubes, called arteries (shown in red). These eventually branch into smaller tubes, called capillaries. They are so narrow that blood cells have to squeeze through in single file. Their walls are only one cell thick, so substances can pass easily through them to and from the blood cells. The capillaries join up again to form veins (shown in blue), which take the blood back to the heart.

Amazing But True

There are about 96,000km (59,520 miles) of blood vessels (arteries, veins and capillaries) in your body. This is enough to stretch almost $2\frac{1}{2}$ times around the Equator. At any time, 75% of your blood is in your veins, 20% in your arteries and 5% in your capillaries.

Amazing artery

The aorta is the largest artery in the body. It is about 2.5cm (1in) wide, 2,500 times wider than most capillaries. It has thick walls which stop blood from leaking out. The walls are stretchy so they bend but do not break under the force of the flowing blood.

What is in blood?

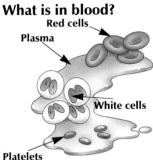

Red cells
Plasma
White cells
Platelets

The main ingredients in blood are:
1. A watery fluid, called plasma. Cells float in it.
2. Red blood cells. These carry oxygen.
3. White blood cells. These fight infection.
4. Platelets. These tiny fragments of cells help your blood clot when you cut yourself.

Red cell life cycle

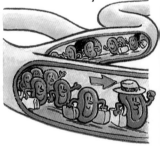

You have about 30 million million red blood cells, more than any other type of cell. They live for about four months. New red cells are made in the bone marrow, at a rate of about 3 million a second. In its short lifetime, a red blood cell will have circulated around your body over 170,000 times.

Not my type

There are different types of blood. Doctors divide them into four main groups – A, B, O and AB. They can do tests to find out which group your blood belongs to. If a person needs a lifesaving blood transfusion, they must be given blood from a suitable group, or they might die. Doctors only discovered the different blood types about 90 years ago.

Under pressure

Your heart pushes the blood along your blood vessels at high pressure. Blood pressure varies around your body. If your blood pressure is too high it can damage your health. Your blood flows along at different speeds. In the aorta, it flows at a speed of 30cm (12in) a second. In the capillaries, it slows to 1cm (0.4in) a second.

DID YOU KNOW?

A teaspoonful of blood contains about 25 million red blood cells, 50,000 white blood cells and 2,500,000 platelets. Red cells are tiny, just 0.007mm (0.0002in) wide. But they are still four times as big as platelets.

Varicose veins

Like your heart, many of your large veins have valves to stop blood from flowing the wrong way. This is particularly important in your legs where blood has to flow uphill. Sometimes the valves fail. Blood flows backward and makes the veins swell up. They are called varicose veins.

Red blooded?

Blood is red because of haemoglobin, a chemical found inside the red blood cells. It absorbs oxygen in the lungs and carries it around the body. Oxygen-rich haemoglobin is bright red. It turns purply blue once it has given up its oxygen load. This is why the veins on the back of your hand look blue.

Main blood vessels

Name of vessel	Function/Details
Aorta	Largest artery in body.
Venae cavae	Main veins back to heart.
Carotid arteries	Carry oxygen to your head.
Jugular veins	Main veins from your head.
Pulmonary artery	Carries blood to lungs to collect oxygen.
Pulmonary vein	Carries oxygen-rich blood from the lungs.
Coronary arteries	Supply heart with its own blood supply.
Femoral arteries and veins	Take blood to and from the legs.

Skin deep

Thick skinned?

In most places, your skin is about 2mm (0.07in) thick. On your eyelids, though, it is just 0.5mm (0.02in) thick. The thickest skin is on the soles of your feet, where it gets the most wear and tear. Here it is 6mm (0.2in) thick. The average thickness of a rhino's skin is 6cm (2.4in), ten times thicker than yours.

A new skin

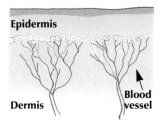

Epidermis

Dermis

Blood vessel

Your skin has two layers – the epidermis and the dermis. The surface of the epidermis is made up of dead skin cells which overlap like roof tiles. They contain a tough protein, called keratin. As they wear out, they are replaced. Living cells deeper in the dermis divide and push the ones above them up. New cells take three weeks to reach the surface.

What does your skin do?

1. Forms a protective barrier against germs, infection, and wear and tear.
2. Protects the body's internal organs from the sun's harmful ultraviolet (UV) rays.
3. Keeps the body's internal temperature steady, at about 37°C (98.6°F), by the processes of sweating, shivering and flushing.
4. Keeps the body waterproof. It also stops precious fluids from being lost and the inside of the body from drying out.
5. Is touch-sensitive.

Goose pimples

Goose pimples are one of your body's ways of trying to warm you up when you get cold. When a furry animal gets cold, its hair stands on end. This traps air next to its skin and keeps it warm. When you get cold, the fine hairs on your body try to stand up too. The muscles that pull each hair up also pull up a tiny bump of skin as a goose pimple.

Fingerprint giveaway

The skin on your fingertips is covered in a pattern of tiny ridges. These are called your fingerprints. Like the treads on the soles of jogging shoes, they help you grip things better. No two people, even identical twins, ever have the same fingerprints. This is why fingerprints are so useful to the police in identifying criminals.

Amazing But True

Household dust is mostly made up of dead skin cells. You lose millions of these every day. In just one year, 2kg (4.4lb) of skin and hair fall off your body.

Cuts ...

If your skin is damaged, it quickly repairs itself. First, your blood clots over the cut and forms a scab. This protects the area until new skin has grown and the wound has healed. Then the scab falls off. You may also need a sticking plaster or a bandage for greater protection.

... and bruises

A hard knock may break some of the blood vessels under your skin. The blood leaks out into the area around the vessels and causes a bruise. A bruise changes colour as the red pigment, haemoglobin, in the blood leaks out and loses the oxygen which gives it its colour. It turns blue then breaks down into other yellow and green pigments.

Skin-deep colour

The colour of your skin depends on how much of the brown-black pigment, called melanin, it contains. Melanin is made by cells, called melanocytes, at the base of the epidermis. Dark skin contains more melanin than light skin. Melanin helps protect the skin from the sun's harmful ultraviolet (UV) rays. This is why your skin may tan in the sun.

In a cold sweat

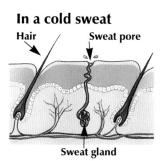

Hair   Sweat pore

Sweat gland

Sweat is a salty liquid made in curly glands deep in the dermis. It oozes to the surface through tiny holes, called pores. As it dries, or evaporates, it draws warmth away from your body and cools you down. You have over 3 million sweat glands. Even on a cool day, you lose 0.3 litres (0.5 pints) of sweat. This rises to 2 litres (3.5 pints) on a hot day.

Under your skin

Deep under your skin, beneath the dermis, is a layer of fat. It acts as an insulator, keeping heat in. It can also be converted into energy by your body. Your fat layer is usually just a few millimetres (about an eighth of an inch) thick. Some whales living in icy seas have fat layers 38cm (15in) thick.

13

Hair and nails

Hairy humans

You have about 5 million hairs on your body, with about 100,000 of these growing on your head. Hair grows out of deep pits, called follicles, in your skin. Cells at the base of the hair divide and push the hair up through the follicle. The hair you can see is made of dead cells, filled with the protein, keratin.

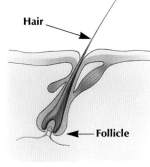

Hair

Follicle

Hair today ...

Your hair grows at a rate of about 2mm (0.08in) a week, or over 10cm (4in) a year. Every two to three years, a hair stops growing and falls out. The follicle then rests for about three months before it produces a new hair. About 70 old hairs fall out every day.

How hair helps

Our ancestors were much hairier than we are. Hair kept them warm. We wear clothes instead. Hair has other functions too. The hairs on your head protect your scalp from the sun. Your eyebrows stop sweat from dripping into your eyes. The surface of each hair is covered in tiny ridges. These help keep dirt and dust off your skin.

Amazing But True

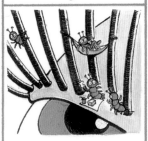

Some people have tiny, harmless, spider-like mites living in the hair follicles of their eyelashes. The mites are just 0.3mm (0.01in) long with four pairs of short legs. They feed on the natural oil, sebum, made in your skin.

Colours and curls

Like the colour of your skin, the colour of your hair depends on how much melanin it contains. Dark hair has lots of melanin; fair hair has very little melanin. The shape of your hair follicles determines whether your hair is straight, wavy or curly. Straight hair grows from a round follicle, wavy hair grows from an oval follicle and curly hair from a flat follicle.

Hair strength

Hair is thinner than paper but it is very strong for its size. In one test a single hair held 170g (6oz), the weight of a large apple. It has been estimated that an adult man of average weight could be lifted up by a rope made of just 100 human hairs. Straight hair is thought to be stronger than curly or wavy hair.

Got an itch?

You may not be able to see what causes an itch, but you can certainly feel the itch itself. An itch may be caused by a speck of dust which has become lodged in a hair follicle, or by a hair bent over inside its follicle. The itchy feeling is detected by tiny, very sensitive nerves around the hair root.

Longest locks

If it is left uncut, hair usually grows to a maximum length of 70cm (27in) before it falls out. In 1949, though, a monk in Madras, India, was reported to have hair 7.92m (26ft) long. This is about 13 times longer than your arm.

Now, your nails

Like skin and hair, nails are mostly made from keratin which makes them hard and tough. Like hair, nails are dead. This is why it does not hurt when you cut them. They grow from a part of the skin, called the nail root. The band of thick skin around the edge of the nail is called the cuticle.

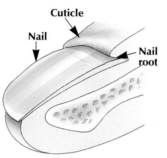

Cuticle

Nail

Nail root

See how they grow

Your fingernails grow 0.05cm (0.02in) a week, four times faster than your toenails. Middle fingernails grow the fastest. Nails grow faster in summer than in winter. Right-handed people have faster-growing nails on their right hands than their left, and vice versa.

DID YOU KNOW?

Because they are dead, nails cannot feel anything on their own. But they help you to touch and feel things by forming tough, firm pads behind your sensitive fingertips. Without their support, your fingertips would bend too much as they tried to touch things.

Half moons

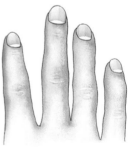

Nails mostly look pink because of the blood vessels in the skin underneath them. The "half moon" shape at the base of each nail looks white because this area is not firmly attached to the skin beneath it.

Brain in charge

Master brain

Your brain controls your body and everything you do, feel and think. It receives information, processes it and decides what action to take, much like a computer. The information travels back and forth along "wires", called nerves. It is thought that the brain can store as much information as a 20-volume encyclopedia.

Brain builders

Your brain looks like a soft, wrinkly, grey lump. It is made up of 10,000 million nerve cells. These are linked in a vast network for sending signals. One cell may be connected to an amazing 200,000 others. Your brain is covered in a mesh of red blood vessels, carried in a tough, protective, skin-like membrane.

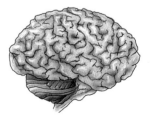

Parts of the brain

Your brain is divided into different parts, each with a different job to do.

Cerebral cortex

Thalamus

Hypothalamus

Cerebellum

Brain stem

Cerebral cortex Controls the senses, intelligence, feelings and movement.
Cerebellum Controls balance and muscle activity.
Brain stem Controls automatic functions, such as your heartbeat and breathing.

Thalamus Sorts messages from the senses. Sends them to the correct part of the brain to be analyzed and acted on.
Hypothalamus Regulates hunger, thirst, your body temperature and also your hormones.

Brain power

The cerebral cortex is the biggest part of the brain. If it were laid out flat, it would cover an area 12 times the size of this page. This is the brain's control area. The cortex is split into two halves, called hemispheres. Each of these is divided into different areas. Some areas deal with messages coming in from the senses. Others deal with outgoing messages.

DID YOU KNOW?

The average human brain weighs about 1.4kg (3lb). This is as much as 13 apples. All adults have brains of a similar size, even geniuses. The heaviest brain of any mammal belongs to the sperm whale. It is six times heavier than a human brain.

On the other hand

Each half of the brain controls the opposite side of the body. In right-handed people, the left side controls writing and speech. In left-handed people, the right side is in charge. About one in ten people are left-handed. Most others are right-handed. A very few people can use both hands equally well. They are called ambidextrous.

Brain food

Your brain is only half the size of your head, but it uses up a fifth of your body's energy supply. It needs a constant supply of blood to provide it with enough oxygen and nutrients. If too little blood reaches your brain, you may feel faint. Your brain cells die after five minutes without oxygen.

A brain of two halves

Each half of your brain deals with different skills and abilities, as shown below. A thick band of nerves, the corpus callosum, joins the two halves.

Right side
Creative and artistic skills, such as playing a musical instrument, drawing and painting. Emotions.

Left side
Logical thought and reasoning, for example in chess playing or computer programming.

What's the matter?

The brain's outer layer is mainly grey matter, with white matter inside. Grey matter consists of nerve cells taking messages from the brain to the body. White matter is made of nerve fibres which regulate the grey matter cells.

Amazing But True

The most brainless animal ever may have been the massive dinosaur, Stegosaurus. It weighed $1\frac{1}{2}$ tonnes ($1\frac{3}{4}$ tons), yet its brain was only the size of a walnut. It made up $\frac{1}{200,000}$ of the dinosaur's body weight. Your brain makes up about $\frac{1}{50}$ of your body weight.

Short-term memory

Your brain stores some information as memories. Long-term memory lasts for years. Short-term memory lasts for about a minute; for instance, the interval between looking up a phone number and making the call.

Memory skills

Some people have better memories than others. A man from Texas, USA, was shown 1,560 playing cards laid out in a random order. He had only one look at them, then the cards were shuffled. Amazingly, he was able to remember all the cards in order, with only two mistakes.

Nerve messengers

Nervous system

Your brain, nerves and spinal cord form your body's nervous system. Your nerves carry messages, in the form of electrical signals, from your body to your brain and from your brain to your body. Your brain controls the whole system and your spinal cord is the main pathway for nerve signals.

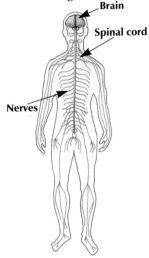

Brain

Spinal cord

Nerves

Taking a back road

Your delicate spinal cord runs down a tunnel of holes in your backbone, or spine. The bones protect it from damage. The cord is a thick bundle of nerves, connecting your brain to the rest of your body. It has 31 pairs of smaller nerves branching off it and reaching every part of the body. In adults, the spinal cord is about 45cm (17.5in) long.

What a nerve!

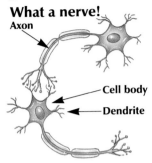

Axon

Cell body

Dendrite

Nerves are made up of bunches of hundreds of long fibres belonging to nerve cells, called neurones. The fibres are called axons. They run from the cell bodies of the neurones. Shorter fibres, or dendrites, also branch off the cell bodies. The axons of one cell join another cell's dendrites or a muscle to pass signals on.

Crossing the gap

The axon of one neurone does not actually touch the dendrites of the next. Nerve signals have to jump across a tiny gap, called a synapse. To get across the gap, they have to change from electrical signals into chemicals, called neurotransmitters. Then they change back into electrical signals.

Amazing But True

An adult has some 75km (46 miles) of nerves, enough to stretch over 185 times around an Olympic running track. The longest single nerve fibre runs from the base of the spine to the tip of the big toe. It can be 1m (3.2ft) long.

Go to sleep ...

If you have an operation, or a filling at the dentist's, you are given an anaesthetic to prevent you from feeling any pain. This is a chemical which stops your nerves from working properly so they cannot pass signals on. A local anaesthetic numbs a particular part of your body, such as your gum. A general anaesthetic puts you into a deep sleep.

What nerves do

There are about 100 million million neurones in your body. They fall into three types:

Type of neurone	Function
Sensory neurone	Carries signals from your sensory organs to your brain.
Motor neurone	Carries signals from your brain to your muscles.
Connector neurone	Passes signals from one cell to the next within your brain and your spinal cord.

Lightning reactions

Some nerve signals travel along your nerves at speeds of about 120m (384ft) a second. This is over 400kph (248mph), faster than a high-speed train. Some signals travel more slowly than others. Pain signals travel more slowly than touch signals. If you stub your toe, you feel the pain about a second after you feel the touch. When you are awake, about 3 million signals flash around your body per second.

Automatic action

A separate set of nerves controls automatic functions, such as breathing, heartbeat, sweating and digestion. They form your autonomic nervous system. It works all of the time.

DID YOU KNOW?

Even before you are born, thousands of your neurones die each day. Luckily you have so many that you do not notice it. Unlike other cells, neurones can never be replaced or repaired. You are born with almost all you will ever have.

Going numb

If you lie on your arm or cross your legs for too long, they may go numb. One reason for this is that the nerves get squashed and cannot pass messages properly. When you take the weight off again, you may get tingling "pins and needles" as the nerves slowly get back to normal and sensation returns to your limbs.

Rapid reflexes

If you accidentally prick your finger on a pin, you pull your hand away at once. This automatic reaction is called a reflex. It is designed to protect you from danger. To do this as quickly as possible, the nerves bypass your brain and go directly to your muscles.

Going to sleep

Time for bed

Your body cannot work all the time without a break. When you sleep, it has a chance to relax and rejuvenate itself. Your brain, too, needs time to rest and sort out information received during the day. Without enough sleep, you soon become confused and unable to concentrate. We spend about a third of our lives asleep.

Keeping time

Your body has a built-in 24-hour clock, which is controlled by a gland in your brain. It tells your body when to sleep and when to wake up. If you fly a long distance, across different time zones, your body clock gets confused. It wants you to go to sleep, even though it may be the middle of the day. This is known as jet lag.

How much sleep do people need?

The amount of sleep people need varies from one person to another. It also depends on age. We seem to need less sleep as we get older. People with the illness, narcolepsy, fall asleep anytime, anywhere.

Type of person	Average amount of sleep needed a day
Newborn baby	16-20 hours
2-year old child	13 hours
5-year old child	10-11 hours
10-year old child	9-10 hours
Adult	7-8 hours
80-year old	5 hours

Amazing But True

People living in parts of Rumania used to think that it was dangerous for a person to sleep with his or her mouth open. They believed that the person's soul, in the shape of a mouse, would run out of the mouth and escape. If the mouse did not return from its travels, the sleeper could never wake up.

Slowing down

When you sleep, your body slows down, but it never stops working completely. Your brain slows down, as do your heart and your breathing

Super snorer

If you sleep on your back, with your mouth open, you may snore. At the back of your throat, where your mouth and nose passages connect, there is a flap of skin called the soft palate. This flap rattles as you breathe out and air rushes past it, making a grunting or snorting sound. The loudest snore so far recorded was louder than a train.

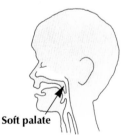

Soft palate

rates. Your muscles relax and your digestive system works more slowly. Your body temperature also drops by about 0.5°C (0.8°F).

DID YOU KNOW?

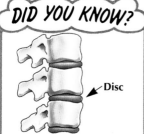

Disc

You grow about 8mm (0.3in) in your sleep, but shrink again during the morning. This is because of the discs of gristly cartilage between the bones in your spine. When you stand or sit up, the discs are squeezed by the force of gravity. When you lie down, the pressure is taken off. The discs expand and make you taller.

Breath of fresh air

You yawn when you are tired, when you wake up, and when you are bored. These are times when you breathe shallowly and do not take in enough oxygen for your body's needs. Yawning is a reflex action which helps get more fresh air into your lungs. You may yawn if you see someone else yawning. It seems to be catching!

Walking in your sleep

No one knows why people talk or walk in their sleep. They are usually sleeping deeply when this happens. Sleep talkers usually mumble and mutter without making much sense. Sleep walkers may try to do everyday tasks, such as making a cup of coffee or going to the toilet.

Sleep cycles

At night, you go through cycles of deep sleep followed by shallow sleep. Each cycle lasts about 90 minutes. In deep sleep, your brain is quiet and relaxed. In shallow sleep, it is more alert and active.

Sweet dreams

Shallow sleep is also called REM sleep. This stands for Rapid Eye Movement. Your eyeballs dart around behind your closed eyelids, as if they are looking around. This is when you dream. No one is sure why, but everyone has about five dreams a night. Dreams are often a mixture of reality and fantasy.

The meaning of dreams

Scientists have many ideas about what dreams may mean. Here are just a few:

Dream	Possible meaning
Flying	Feeling confident.
Falling	Fear of failure, for example in a school test or exam.
Taking an exam or test	Unsolved problems at home, school or work.
Being naked	Feeling insecure or vulnerable.
Being chased	Feeling worried or under pressure.

Your senses

Keeping informed

Your senses tell you what is happening in the outside world. Your five main senses are sight, smell, taste, hearing and touch. Each has a sense organ, connected by nerves to your brain. Your eyes see, your nose smells, your tongue tastes, your ears hear and your skin feels.

The parts of your eye

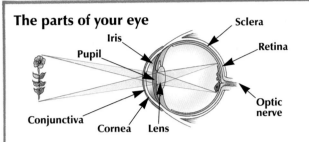

Conjunctiva Clear protective layer.
Cornea Clear layer which helps focus the image.
Lens Disc which focuses the image. Also turns the image upside down. Your brain turns the image the right way up again.

Iris Coloured part of the eye.
Pupil Hole in the middle of the iris where light rays enter.
Retina Area at the back with nerve cells.
Optic nerve Main nerve from eye to brain.
Sclera The "white" of the eye.

Seeing sense

You see things because light rays bounce off objects and enter your eyes. The front part of your eye projects the rays on to the back of your eye, where they form an upside-down image. Here they hit nerve cells which send signals to your brain. An area at the back of your brain sorts the signals out and puts them together as the picture you see.

Rods and cones

The light-sensitive nerve cells in the retina are called rods and cones. Each eye has about 125 million rods and 7 million cones. Rods only detect black and white but they work well in dim light. Cones see colours but can only work in bright light. At night, you see mainly in shades of grey because only your rods can work in the poor light.

DID YOU KNOW?

Some people have faulty cone cells and cannot see colours properly. About one in 20 people are red-green colour blind. They have problems telling the difference between shades of red and green. About one in 40,000 people cannot see colours at all. They only see in black, white and grey.

Blue eyes, brown eyes

The coloured part of your eye, the iris, gets its name from Iris, the Ancient Greek goddess of the rainbow. Your eye colour depends on how much of the brown pigment, melanin, your irises contain. Melanin also colours skin and hair. You inherit your colouring from your parents.

Pupil power

Your pupils can change size depending on the amount of light coming into your eyes. Muscles around your irises make your pupils smaller in bright light so you are not dazzled. In dim light, the muscles make the pupils wider so they can take in as much light as possible.

Amazing But True

Carrots can help you see in the dark. They provide a source of Vitamin A which makes the light-sensitive chemical in your rods. In World War II, the British wanted to keep their radar equipment secret. They claimed that their pilots could see and fly in the dark because they ate a lot of carrots.

Seeing straight

Some people have eyeballs which cannot focus light properly. Near-sighted people cannot see distant objects very well. They have long eyeballs which make light rays fall short of the retina.

Near sight

Long-sighted* people have short eyeballs so rays fall behind the retina. They cannot see close things clearly.

Long sight

*Farsighted (US)

How do you smell?

Smells are tiny amounts of chemicals in the air. When you breathe in, smells go up your nose and into a hollow space, called the nasal cavity. They are picked up by smell detector cells which have tiny hairs on them, covered in sticky mucus. It absorbs the smell chemicals. Then the cells send signals to your brain.

Smell cells

Your smell receptor cells cover an area only about the size of a postage stamp. Yet they allow you to detect over 3,000 smells. An Alsatian dog's nose, however, is so sensitive that it can smell about a million times better than that.

A good sniff

Things smell stronger if you sniff their scent. When you breathe in normally, only a small amount of air and smells float into your nasal cavity. When you sniff hard, you direct a long stream of air toward your smell detectors.

23

Taste sensation

Your tongue is a piece of flexible muscle. It helps you talk and break up your food. It also allows you to taste your food, by detecting tiny amounts of chemicals in it. They dissolve in the saliva, or spit, you make in your mouth. Signals about the tastes travel along nerves to your brain.

Budding tasters

Your tongue is covered in tiny taste buds, lined with special taste-sensitive cells. These detect four main tastes – sweet, sour, salty and bitter. You have over 10,000 taste buds but they decrease in number as you get older. Different parts of your tongue pick up different flavours. For example, the tip detects saltiness.

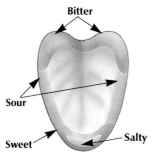

Bitter

Sour

Sweet — Salty

Journey through your ear

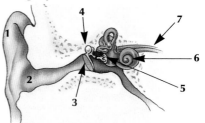

1. Earflap Funnels sounds into ear.
2. Ear canal Sounds travel down tube-like canal to ear drum.
3. Ear drum Membrane across ear canal. Sounds make it vibrate.
4. Ear bones Tiny bones pick up the vibrations.

5. Oval window Another membrane. Vibrates when ear bones vibrate.
6. Cochlea Curled tube, filled with liquid. Vibrations shake liquid which pulls on nerve endings.
7. Auditory nerve The nerve endings send signals along this nerve to the brain.

DID YOU KNOW?

Your senses of taste and smell are closely linked. If you have a cold and your nose is stopped up, all your food will probably taste the same. This is because your sense of smell cannot pick up delicate flavours as efficiently as usual. Your sense of smell is 10,000 times more sensitive than your sense of taste.

Hear, hear!

Your ears can pick up sounds as loud as a jet aircraft and as quiet as a whisper. The object making the sound causes the air around it to vibrate. Your ears are designed to pick up these vibrations, which are called sound waves.

High and low notes

High sounds are caused by the air vibrating very quickly. Low sounds are made by the air vibrating slowly. In a low rumble, the air vibrates about 20 times a second. In a very high note, it vibrates 20,000 times a second. Your cochlea picks up the different vibrations.

In a spin

If you spin around and around, then stop, you may feel dizzy. This is because the fluid in your semi-circular canals is still swirling around even though your body is standing still. Your brain gets confused by the conflicting messages from your ears and from your muscles.

DID YOU KNOW?

Your skin is not equally sensitive all over. Some areas have more nerve cells. The most sensitive skin is on your fingertips, toes and lips. There are 20 times more cold detectors in your lips, for example, than in your legs. Your least sensitive skin is on your back and bottom.

Well balanced

Your ears also help you to keep your balance. In each ear you have three fluid-filled tubes. These are called semi-circular canals. They contain sense cells. If you move your head, the fluid in the canals moves and triggers the sense cells. They tell your brain about the new position of your head. Balance is sometimes called the sixth sense.

Sensitive skin

There are millions of sensitive nerve cells packed under the surface of your skin. Each type of nerve cell detects a different kind of sensation. Your skin can detect light touches and heavy pressure, hard and soft textures, and heat and cold. It can also detect pain. Pain warns your body of possible damage.

Seeing with skin

Blind people use their sense of touch to help them read. They use a special alphabet, called braille. It consists of patterns of raised bumps printed on paper. Series of bumps represent words or letters. Blind people feel these with their fingertips. Braille was invented by a blind Frenchman, Louis Braille, in 1824.

Your lungs and breathing

The need to breathe

You need to breathe to get oxygen from the air into your body. Your cells use oxygen to release energy from food. Without a constant supply, they would die in a few minutes. Your cells also make a waste gas, carbon dioxide, which you breathe out. The process of breathing is called respiration.

Breathing know-how

Air goes in through your nose, then down your trachea (windpipe), then down two tubes, called bronchi, into your lungs. The bronchi branch into tubes which end in air sacs (alveoli), which are covered in blood vessels. Oxygen seeps from the sacs into the blood and is carried around your body to your cells.

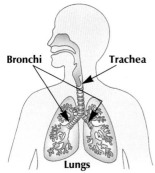

Bronchi **Trachea**

Lungs

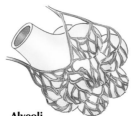

Alveoli

You have about 300 million alveoli (air sacs) in each lung. They give your lungs a huge surface for absorbing oxygen from the air you breathe in. If the alveoli were spread out flat, they could cover an area the size of a tennis court.

In and out

When you breathe in, your chest muscles pull your ribs up and out. Your diaphragm, the muscle under your chest, moves down. Your chest expands and your lungs fill with air. When you breathe out, the muscles relax. Your ribs move down, and your diaphragm moves up to squeeze air out.

Lung volume

In a normal breath, you take in about 0.5 litres (0.8 pints) of air. If you are exercising, you may take in ten times as much air to supply your hard-working muscles with extra oxygen. When full, your lungs hold about 3 litres (5 pints) of air. In a day, an adult breathes enough air to fill a thousand party balloons.

Air amounts

Each minute, a new-born baby breathes a total of 0.5 litres (0.8 pints) of air in and out. A sprinting athlete breathes about 70 litres (123 pints) of air a minute, 140 times as much as a baby.

Breathing rates

You breathe all the time, automatically. But your breathing rate depends on your age and on what you are doing.

Category	Breaths per minute
Newborn baby	14-60
Young child	35
Adult man/woman	12-18
Sleeping adult	12-14
Sprinting athlete	25

Speedy sneezes

Sneezing helps clear slimy mucus or dust from your nose. You inhale deeply and shut off your nose and throat so that air pressure builds up in your lungs. When the pressure is too great, the air bursts out of your nose. You normally breathe air out at about 8kph (5mph). In a sneeze, air travels at over 160kph (99mph).

Hic! Hic! Hic!

Hiccups are short, sudden gasps of breath. They happen when your diaphragm contracts and moves down more sharply than usual. After each breath your vocal cords snap shut, making a "hic" noise. Frightening the sufferer or drinking from the wrong side of a glass are among the many supposed cures for hiccups.

Coughs and colds

Like sneezing, coughing is an automatic reaction which helps to clear mucus or dust out of the breathing passages in your lungs. But coughs and sneezes spread diseases. If you have a cold, the air you cough or sneeze out contains millions of cold germs. If other people breathe these germs in, they may catch cold too.

The high life

The higher up you go, the lower the amount of oxygen in the air and the more difficult it is to breathe. Mountaineers often have to use oxygen masks. The Quechua Indians live 3,650m (12,000ft) up in the Andes in South America. To help them breathe more easily, they have larger hearts and lungs which can carry more oxygen than normal.

DID YOU KNOW?

You cannot usually see the air you breathe out. But on cold days the air you exhale is visible. This is because your breath contains water vapour, as well as carbon dioxide. As the water vapour meets cold air, it condenses and turns into tiny droplets of liquid water which look like white puffs of steam.

Speaking volumes

Lump in your throat

If you look in a mirror and swallow, you will see a lump in your throat. This is your larynx, or voice box. It sits at the top of your trachea, or windpipe. Two bands of elastic tissue and muscle are stretched across it. These are your vocal cords. When you speak, you breathe out and air passes over the cords. It makes them vibrate and produce sounds.

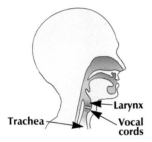

Trachea — Larynx — Vocal cords

Perfect pitch

Muscles in your voice box alter the shape of your vocal cords to produce high and low sounds. High sounds are made when the cords are taut. Low notes are made when they are looser. The harder you breathe out when you speak or sing, the louder the sound you will make.

High notes

Low notes

Voice breaking

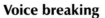

The size of your voice box and your vocal cords affects how deep your voice is. In his early teens, a boy's voice gets deeper or "breaks". This is because his vocal cords grow twice as fast as a girl's. When you are born, your vocal cords are about 6mm (0.2in) long. They grow to 20mm (0.8in) in adult women and 30mm (1.2in) in adult men.

Shaping sounds

Your lips, teeth, tongue, cheeks and throat muscles help you shape different sounds into words. This is why it is so difficult to speak with your mouth shut. The different parts are all controlled by the speech centre in your brain.

A bird does not shape sounds with its mouth, as you do. Birds do not have vocal cords, but make sounds with their voice boxes alone. Tiny muscles pull to create all the different bird sounds. This is why birds can sing with closed beaks.

Prehistoric talk

Scientists think that, until about 40,000 years ago, people's skulls and voice boxes were not the right shape to make the sort of sounds we use today. People probably used grunts and gestures to talk to each other. The scientists did research on plaster casts they made of prehistoric skulls.

Turning up the volume

The volume, or loudness, of sounds is measured in units called decibels (dB). The softest sound you can hear is about 10dB. Sounds above 90dB can damage your hearing. The list below gives you the decibel level of some of the sounds people make.

Sound	Decibel level
Whispering	30-40dB
Normal talking	60dB
Loud talking	70dB
Opera singer	80-90dB
Loudest recorded snore	90dB
Rock concert	100dB
Loudest recorded shout	119dB
Loudest recorded whistle	122.5dB
Loudest recorded scream	128dB

Tonsils on guard

Your tonsils are two fleshy pads on either side of your throat. They guard your throat against infection from airborne germs. Your tonsils contain millions of white blood cells which destroy the germs which spread diseases. Tonsils can sometimes become swollen with infection but usually shrink back to normal size.

Sound sinuses

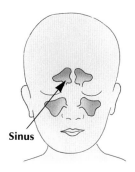

Sinus

Your sinuses are air-filled hollows inside the bones of your skull. There is a pair in your forehead and a pair in your cheeks. They are linked to your breathing passages and help to warm the air you breathe in. When you speak, the air in your sinuses vibrates. This helps to make your voice sound clearer and more varied in tone. If you have a cold and your sinuses are blocked, your voice sounds very flat.

Amazing But True

People on La Gomera, in the Canary Islands, mainly speak Spanish. But they also use a whistled language, called silbo, to talk to each other. On a clear day, the sound can carry up to 8km (5 miles). This is useful because the island is very hilly and it is quicker to whistle to people living in the next valley than to walk over to see them.

Speed speaking

Most people find it difficult to speak clearly at over 300 words a minute. One of the fastest talkers was a radio commentator, Raymond Glendinning. He once spoke 176 words in 30 seconds while reporting on a greyhound race.

Digesting your food

Food travels

As food travels through you, it is broken into particles small enough to be absorbed into your blood. This is called digestion.

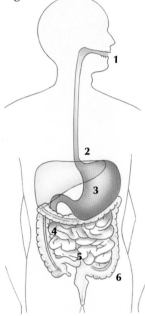

Amazing But True

During digestion, food travels through about 9m (29.5ft) of pipes and tubes inside your body, a distance as long as three cars. Your small intestine alone is 4m (13ft) long. It is coiled up inside your abdomen. It is "small" only because it is just 4cm (1.5in) wide. Your large intestine is three times as wide but only 1.5m (5ft) long.

1. Your teeth and tongue chop and mash the food. It is mixed with saliva.
2. The food goes down your oesophagus (gullet) into your stomach.
3. Digestive juices break the food down into a creamy mixture.
4. The mixture goes down your small intestine. More juices are added.
5. The food is absorbed into your blood through the wall of your small intestine.
6. Any unabsorbed food goes into the large intestine and then out of your body as faeces.

Stomach stay

A meal may take up to three days to pass through your digestive system. It spends about three hours in your stomach. Your stomach is a stretchy, muscular bag. When it is full, it can hold about 15 cupfuls of liquid.

Going the wrong way

Your oesophagus and your trachea (windpipe) are next to each other in your throat. A flap, called the epiglottis, usually covers the top of your trachea when you swallow. But food may still sometimes go down your trachea by mistake and make you choke.

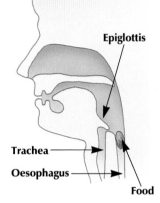

Epiglottis

Trachea

Oesophagus

Food

Choppers and chewers

Your teeth chop and chew your food to make it easier to swallow. You are born without teeth. By the age of about two, you have your first set of 20 "milk" teeth. When you are about six, your adult teeth begin to push your milk teeth out. There are 32 teeth in a full adult set.

Food does not just slip down your digestive tube. It is pushed along by a process called peristalsis. The muscles in the tube-walls squeeze behind the food and push it forward, in the same way as you squeeze toothpaste out of a tube. Peristalsis means that you can still eat or drink even if you are standing on your head.

Liver aside

Before it goes to the rest of your body, your blood carries digested food to your liver. It stores some nutrients and changes others into more useful forms. Your liver also makes a green liquid, called bile. It helps to break down fats as food passes through your small intestine. The bile is stored in your gall bladder until it is needed.

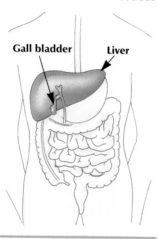

Gall bladder   Liver

Feeling hungry?

In your lifetime, you eat about 30 tonnes (29½ tons) of food, equal in weight to six elephants. Food provides you with energy to keep your body working and nutrients for repair and growth. Feeling hungry is your body's way of telling you that supplies are low.

Calorie counting

Energy from food is measured in kilocalories (KCals) or kilojoules (KJoules). One KCal equals 4.2 KJoules. An apple contains about 50KCals. This provides enough energy for you to swim for five minutes. You could swim for 30 minutes on the energy in a chocolate bar.

A balanced diet

Different foods contain different nutrients. You need a mixture to stay healthy and grow.

Nutrient and use in body	Examples of foods it is found in
Protein (growth, repair)	Lean meat, fish, milk nuts, beans
Carbohydrate (energy)	Bread, potatoes, rice, sugar
Fat (energy, warmth)	Butter, milk, oil, cheese, fatty meats
Fibre (healthy digestion)	Bran, whole wheat bread, fruit, vegetables
Vitamins and minerals (regulate chemical processes in body)	Fruit, vegetables, fish, milk, eggs

Getting rid of waste

Body wastes

Digestion, respiration and the chemical processes happening inside your body all make waste products which have to be eliminated. Your body wastes include faeces, carbon dioxide, water, urine and sweat.

Solid extras

During digestion, solid wastes from your food pass through your large intestine and into your rectum. They are stored until they leave your body as faeces when you go to the toilet. Faeces also contain water, dead bacteria that were used to kill germs in your food, dead cells that lined your intestine, and mucus.

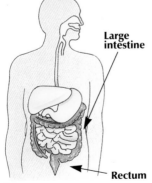

Large intestine

Rectum

Kind kidneys

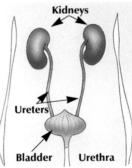

Kidneys

Ureters

Bladder   Urethra

Your two kidneys clean your blood and get rid of wastes. They contain about a million tiny filters, or nephrons. The waste liquid from your kidneys is called urine. It flows down two tubes, called ureters, into your bladder. When you go to the toilet, it flows out through another tube, called the urethra. A man's urethra is about five times longer than a woman's because it has to reach to the end of his penis.

Useful urine

About 96% of urine is water. It also contains some waste salts and a substance called urea. Urea is made during the breakdown of proteins in your liver. Urea may also leave your body in sweat. If urea builds up in your body, it is a sign that your kidneys are not working properly. Kidney failure can be fatal if it is not treated quickly.

Free flow

Until you are about two years old, you pass urine as a reflex action. It happens automatically when your bladder is full. As you get older, you learn how to control your bladder. Some people lose this control again when they get very old.

Baggy bladder

Your bladder is like a muscular bag which stretches as it fills up with urine. When it is full, it can hold nearly the same amount of liquid as two cans of drink. But you would be desperate for a toilet by this time! A tight band of muscle around the neck of your bladder keeps the urine in. When this muscles relaxes, the urine flows out down the urethra.

Amazing But True

About 150 litres (33 gallons) of fluid pass through your kidneys every day. But 99% of this is cleaned and goes back into your blood. In their lifetimes, adults pass about 40,000 litres (8,800 gallons) of urine. This is enough to fill 500 baths.

Fluids in balance

Apart from getting rid of wastes, your kidneys control the balance of fluids in your body. If you take in more liquid than you need, they make more urine to get rid of the excess. The list shows how much liquid goes in and out of your body in an average day:

Water in	Water out
1.5 litres (2.6 pints) from food and drink	0.7 litres (1.2 pints) in urine and faeces
	0.5 litres (0.9 pints) in sweat
	0.3 litres (0.5 pints) in breathed-out air
Total = 1.5 litres (2.6 pints)	**Total** = 1.5 litres (2.6 pints)

Stony kidneys

If your kidneys do not get enough liquid passing through them, the urine they make may be too concentrated. The solids in it may join together to form kidney "stones". If the stones are bigger than peas, they can block the ureters and cause terrible pain. Kidney stones have even been found inside the bodies of Ancient Egyptian mummies.

Pollution control

Your liver gets rid of waste by a process called detoxification. It turns toxic, or poisonous, substances into harmless ones. Toxic substances are found in some foods and in alcoholic drinks. It takes the liver about an hour to absorb the alcohol in just one glass of wine. People who regularly drink too much overwork their livers. This can cause the liver disease, cirrhosis, which can be fatal.

Chemicals in control

Keeping control

Your brain is in overall control of your body. But it uses two different systems for sending messages around your body. One system is the nervous system. This uses electrical signals for quick reactions. The other is the endocrine system. This system uses chemical messengers, called hormones. They usually work more slowly.

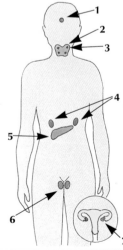

DID YOU KNOW?

Your body makes over 20 types of hormones. They are released into your bloodstream by the glands that make them and are carried around your body by your blood. Each type of hormone affects a different part of your body, called its target organ. The hormone can adjust the speed at which this organ works, or turn it on or off.

Master gland

Your pituitary gland is about the size of a pea. It hangs down from the base of your brain by a short stalk. It is the most important endocrine gland in your body. Five of the 11 hormones it produces are used to control the actions of the other glands. In turn, however, the pituitary gland is controlled by the hypothalamus at the base of your brain.

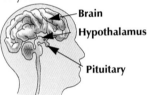

Brain

Hypothalamus

Pituitary

Glands and hormones

Hormones are made in groups of cells, called endocrine glands. Your main glands are shown below:

Gland	Main hormones	Functions
1. Pituitary	Include growth hormone, prolactin.	Controls other endocrine glands, growth, mother's milk production.
2. Thyroid	Thyroxine	Controls use of energy by body (metabolism).
3. Parathyroids – behind the thyroid.	Parathormone (parathyroid)	Regulates calcium levels in blood and bones.
4. Adrenals	Adrenaline, aldosterone	Controls blood pressure, muscles, body's salt level.
5. Pancreas	Insulin	Controls use of sugar by body.
6. Testicles – in a male's scrotum.	Testosterone	Controls sexual development in males.
7. Ovaries – in a female's abdomen.	Oestrogen, progesterone	Controls sexual development in females.

Getting bigger

The pituitary gland produces the hormone which controls growth. You grow faster at night because more hormone is released into your blood when you are asleep. If too much growth hormone is made, a person may be much taller than normal. The tallest person known was an American, Robert Wadlow. He was 2.72m (8ft 11in) tall when he died in 1940.

Speedy or slow

The hormone, thyroxine, made by your thyroid gland, controls the use of energy by your body. This is known as your metabolic rate. If your thyroid makes too much thyroxine, you may be very active and thin. If it makes too little hormone, you may feel sluggish and put on weight easily.

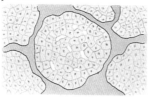
Pancreas purposes

Your pancreas is a thin, triangular gland, about 15cm (5.8in) long. It makes insulin which controls the level of sugar in your blood. Insulin is made in small cell clusters, called Islets of Langerhans, shown below. There are about one million islets in your pancreas. Your pancreas also makes digestive juices.

Diabetes danger

If the pancreas does not make enough insulin, people might suffer from the disease, diabetes. This can cause tiredness and weight loss. Some people with diabetes have daily injections of insulin. This is usually human insulin, made in a laboratory by genetic engineering. They also have to control their sugar intake.

Sex hormones

The male testicles make testosterone. This hormone gives men their male characteristics, such as hair on their faces and bodies. It also controls the production of sperm cells, needed to make babies. The female ovaries make oestrogen and progesterone. These prepare women's bodies for having babies. They also give women their female characteristics, such as breasts.

Being born

Getting together

For a baby to form, a sperm cell from a man must join with a woman's egg cell, or ovum. This is called fertilization. The egg is made in one of the woman's ovaries. It then travels down a tube, called a Fallopian tube. During sexual intercourse, the man's sperm pass into the woman's body and swim up into the tube where fertilization may occur.

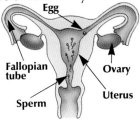

Egg

Fallopian tube

Ovary

Uterus

Sperm

Stages of development

After fertilization, the new cell divides until it forms a ball of at least 64 cells. Then it embeds itself in the lining of the mother's uterus, or womb. Over the next 9 months it grows and develops into a baby.

Month	Development of baby inside womb
1	Heart begins to beat.
2	Has tiny hands and feet. Has eyes but no eyelids.
3	Looks more like a miniature person.
4	Can now swallow and pass urine. Has fingernails and toenails.
5	Hairs, eyebrows and eyelashes grow.
6	Sleeps and wakes up at regular times.
7	Moves in the womb. May get hiccups.
8	Lungs develop. Sucks thumb in preparation for sucking mother's milk.
9	Turns head-down, ready to be born.

DID YOU KNOW?

Egg cells are the biggest human cells. Ten would fit across a pinhead. Sperm cells look like tadpoles, with long tails to help them swim to the egg. It would take about 400 sperm (minus tails) to fit across a pinhead. A man makes millions of sperm a day. A woman usually makes one egg a month.

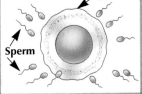

Egg

Sperm

At a stretch

The mother's uterus is made of strong muscle. It has to stretch as the baby grows inside it. It is normally the size and shape of a pear. During pregnancy, it stretches to almost twice the size of a soccer ball. It returns to almost its normal size six weeks after the birth.

Life support

In the uterus, the baby gets food and oxygen from an organ called the placenta. It brings the mother's and baby's blood close together, although they never mix. Food and oxygen pass across the placenta and into the baby's blood through its umbilical cord. Waste products go the other way. Your belly button shows where your umbilical cord was.

Blood boom

During pregnancy, the amount of blood in a mother's body may increase by a third from about 4 litres (7 pints) to 5.5 litres (9.6 pints). This extra blood is needed to supply the growing baby with nourishment and oxygen. The mother's heart has to work harder to pump the blood around her body.

Amazing But True

The most babies ever born to one mother is said to be 69. Between 1725-1765, the wife of a Russian peasant gave birth to 16 pairs of twins, seven sets of triplets and four sets of quadruplets.

Boys and girls

Inside your cells are tiny threads, called chromosomes. These carry instructions for your characteristics. You inherit 23 chromosomes from each parent. Your sex is determined by those known as X and Y chromosomes. All eggs carry X chromosomes. Half the sperm carry an X and half carry a Y. If an egg and an X sperm join, a girl develops. An egg and a Y sperm form a boy.

Blue genes?

The instructions in your chromosomes are called genes. Half come from your mother and half from your father. Genes determine your physical characteristics, your blood group and other features. Some genes are dominant over others. If one of your parents has brown eyes and the other blue, you will probably have brown eyes because brown genes are dominant over blue.

Seeing double?

There is about a one in 80 chance of a mother having twins. There are two types of twins. If two egg cells join with two separate sperm, non-identical* twins will be born. They each have different chromosomes so they can be of different sexes. Identical twins are born when a fertilized egg splits into two and each half develops into a baby. The twins look the same because they have identical chromosomes.

Identical twins share a placenta. Non-identical* twins have one each.

Test-tube baby

If a mother has blocked Fallopian tubes, sperm cannot reach the egg to make a baby. Doctors can now remove the egg and fertilize it with sperm in a laboratory. When the fertilized cell starts to divide, it is placed in the mother's womb to grow into a baby. The world's first "test-tube" baby was born in July 1978.

*fraternal (US)

Growing up

Baby brain

A newborn baby's head looks huge in comparison to its body. Its head alone makes up a quarter of its total length. This is because its brain is already very well developed. By its second birthday, its brain is almost adult size. As the child grows up, the proportions of its body change. By the time it is an adult, its head only makes up an eighth of its total height.

Soft spots

A newborn baby has soft patches of membrane between its skull bones. These are fontanelles. They allow the baby's head to change shape so it can squeeze out of its mother's body more easily. The head returns to a normal shape a few days later. The fontanelles shrink and close over the next two years, to be replaced by bone.

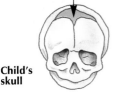

Fontanelle

Child's skull

DID YOU KNOW?

Most babies are about 50cm (19.5in) tall at birth. A baby's height increases by about half in its first year. At 18 months old, a girl is about half her adult height. A boy is about half his adult height at two years old. A seven-year old girl is about three-quarters her adult height. A boy reaches this stage at the age of nine.

More muscle

As you grow up, your muscles get bigger and you get stronger. At birth, your muscles make up about 20% of your weight. In your early teens this increases to 25%. In adults, muscles make up about 40% of their total weight. Men tend to have bigger muscles than women.

Rates of growth

You keep growing until you are about 20 years old. You grow very fast for the first two years, then more steadily until you are about ten, when you shoot up again.

Age (years)	Sex	Average height
0	Boy/Girl	50cm (19.5in)
2	Girl	86.5cm (34in)
2	Boy	87cm (34.2in)
7	Girl	122cm (48in)
7	Boy	122.4cm (48.1in)
13	Girl	154cm (60.6in)
13	Boy	153cm (60.2in)
16	Girl	162cm (63.7in)
16	Boy	171cm (67.3in)
20	Girl	163cm (64.1in)
20	Boy	175cm (68.8in)

Time for a change

Between the ages of 11-18, you change from a child into an adult. This time is known as adolescence. It begins with a stage called puberty. This is when your body starts to grow up and change. Girls go through puberty when they are about 11, boys when they are about 13.

Life expectancy

After adolescence, your body slowly begins to age. But people in wealthier countries, such as Britain and the USA, are now living much longer because of better diets, more exercise and less risk of infection. In 1800, men usually lived for 47 years and women for 51 years. Men now live for about 73 years and women for 76.

How puberty changes you

The physical changes which happen at puberty prepare your body for being grown up and having babies. These are the main changes:

Boys	Girls
Grow taller.	Grow taller.
Moustache and beard start to grow.	Breasts grow.
Voice "breaks" and gets deeper.	Underarm and pubic hair grows.
Underarm and pubic hair grows.	Hips get wider.
	Periods start.

Growing old

As people reach the age of 55-60, their bodies take longer to repair themselves. Their skin may wrinkle and their senses become less sharp. People also shrink as they get older. At the age of 75, they may be 7.6cm (3in) shorter than they were at the age of 20. This is because the discs of cartilage between their backbones shrink and shorten their spines.

Going grey

Amazing But True

The oldest person on record was Shigechiyo Izumi of Japan. He died in February 1986 at the grand old age of 120 years and 237 days. The chances of a person living to the age of 115 years are thought to be only about one in 2.1 million million.

As people get older, the amount of pigment (melanin) available to colour their hair gets less and less until only grey or white hairs are made. These do not contain melanin. Their colour is solely due to the protein, keratin, which hair is made of.

Body repairs

Infection invasion

Most illnesses are called infections. They are caused by tiny living things, often called germs. These may be bacteria, viruses, protozoa or fungi. They invade your body through your nose or mouth, or through cuts or scrapes. Inside you, they multiply and attack your cells. You get symptoms such as aching bones, fever, rashes and sickness as your body fights back.

Amazing But True

Bacteria   **Viruses**

Germs are too small to see except under a powerful microscope. It would take millions of viruses to cover a pinhead. Bacteria are bigger than viruses. But it would still take over a thousand to cover a pinhead.

Germ attack

There are thousands of different types of germs. Each causes a particular type of illness, such as the ones shown below.

Germ group	Types of illness
Bacteria	Tonsilitis; food poisoning; whooping cough; tuberculosis; pneumonia; tetanus
Viruses	Common cold; influenza (flu); chicken pox; measles; mumps; rubella; polio; AIDS
Protozoa	Malaria; sleeping sickness; amoebic dysentery
Fungi	Athlete's foot; ringworm

Spreading out

Germs can be spread by air, water, food and by animal carriers such as mosquitoes. The latter spread the tiny protozoa which cause malaria in tropical countries. The mosquitoes suck the blood of an infected person, then transfer the germs into the next person they attack. Up to 400 million people a year suffer from malaria. The disease kills about 2,750 children a day.

Cancer cells

Some serious illnesses may not be caused by germs. Cancer is caused by cells going out of control and multiplying, destroying healthy cells.

Common complaints

The two most common infections are the common cold and gum disease, such as gingivitis. This disease makes your gums red and swollen and can lead to tooth decay. Scientists estimate that about 80% of people suffer from gum disease at some point in their lives.

The most common cancers affect the lungs, liver, breasts, intestines, blood and skin. Some are cured with drugs, X-ray treatment or surgery.

Self-defence mechanisms

Your body has many ways of defending itself from germs. Firstly your skin tries to keep germs out. But if they do get inside, your body has several methods of fighting back.

Body part	Function
Skin	Forms germ-proof barrier.
Nose	Hairs and mucus trap germs and dirt from the air.
Ears	Wax inside traps germs.
Eyelids	Keep germs out of eyes.
Tears	Wash eyes clean.
Stomach	Juices kill germs in food.
Tonsils and adenoids	Kill germs in your throat.
White blood cells	Destroy germs inside body.
Spleen	Contains white blood cells which fight infection.

Lymph flow

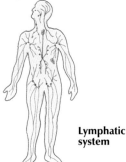

Lymphatic system

Some of the liquid in your blood is constantly seeping out of the blood vessels into another network of tubes, called the lymphatic system. This fluid is called lymph. It carries germ-fighting white blood cells around your body. It drains back into your blood in your chest.

Cell soldiers

Your white blood cells are your most important defence against germs. There are two types of white cell soldiers. The phagocytes surround and eat up harmful germs. The lymphocytes make chemicals, called antibodies. These stick on to germs and kill them. The thousands of different antibodies are each designed to kill one type of germ. Your lymphocytes can produce an amazing 2,000 antibodies a second.

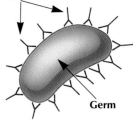

Antibodies

Germ

Fooled again

Once your lymphocytes have made an antibody, they can make it again very quickly and kill the germs before the illness takes hold. This makes you resistant, or immune, to the disease. Your body can be fooled into becoming immune by being given a mild dose of germs, by injection or drops. This is called immunization. Your body makes its antibodies, giving you immunity.

DID YOU KNOW?

The lymph tubes in your neck, armpits and groin form clusters, or nodes. These make white blood cells. They are usually the size of kidney beans. But if you are ill, they make extra cells and can swell to the size of golf balls.

41

Medical marvels

Miracle mould

Penicillium mould

Penicillin and other antibiotic drugs are widely used to treat infections caused by bacteria. Penicillin was only discovered in 1928. A Scottish scientist, Alexander Fleming, found that a type of mould, penicillium, could kill germs. Penicillin, derived from penicillium, is used to treat illnesses such as pneumonia which were once fatal.

DID YOU KNOW?

An American dentist, Horace Wells, used the first anaesthetics in 1844. Before this, patients were held down during operations or made drunk. In 1847, a woman was given chloroform to lessen the pain of childbirth. She was so pleased with the result that she named her daughter Anaesthesia.

Vital vaccines

Vaccines are mild doses of disease-causing germs, which make you immune to diseases.

Disease	Vaccine discovered by	Date
Smallpox	Edward Jenner (GB)	1796
Cholera	Louis Pasteur (France)	1879
Rabies	Louis Pasteur (France)	1885
Tuberculosis	Calmette/Guérin (France)	1924
Polio	Jonas Salk (USA)	1954
Measles	John Enders (USA)	1960
Rubella	Thomas Weller (USA)	1962

Saved from smallpox

Despite being discovered in 1796, Jenner's smallpox vaccine did not become widely available for many years. Smallpox killed millions of people. Thanks to a worldwide vaccination effort, however, the last case of smallpox was reported in 1977 and the disease declared extinct in 1980.

Plant painkiller

Aspirin is one of the most commonly taken medicines of all. It belongs to a group of drugs called analgesics. These help to ease aches and pains. Today aspirins are made from synthetic (man-made) chemicals. But the drug was originally found in the bark of the white willow tree and in the meadowsweet plant.

Pins and needles?

Acupuncture is a type of treatment which relieves pain without using drugs. It was first used in China 5,000 years ago. Fine needles are pushed into points on your body which lie on invisible lines, called meridians. The pressure of the needles on the lines eases the pain. Although the needles may be up to 8cm (3in) long, they do not hurt.

White willow   **Meadowsweet**

Medical specialists

Some doctors specialize in particular aspects of medicine. Here you can find out what some of their titles mean.

Doctor's title	Speciality
Anaesthetist	Anaesthetic drugs
Cardiologist	Heart diseases
Dermatologist	Skin diseases
Geriatrician	Medicine for the elderly
Haematologist	Blood disorders
Orthopaedic surgeon	Bone and joint problems
Paediatrician	Children's illnesses
Pharmacist	Medicines and drugs
Psychiatrist	Mental illnesses
Radiologist	Using X-rays

See-through body

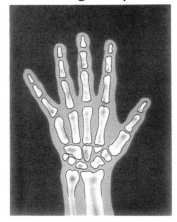

X-rays are used to look inside your body and take photographs of it. X-rays are invisible rays of energy. They can pass through soft flesh but not through hard bones. The flesh shows up black and the bones white. X-rays were first discovered by a German scientist, Wilhelm Röntgen, in 1895. He named them "X-rays" because of their mysterious nature.

Amazing But True

Doctors used to think that the heart was the body's centre of intelligence, not the brain. In 1628, however, William Harvey discovered that the heart pumped blood around the body. Many people found this very hard to believe. It took another 150 years before scientists finally realized what the brain's real function was in the body.

An ear to the heart

Doctors use stethoscopes to listen to the heart and lungs. The first one was made in 1816 by a French doctor, René Laënnec. He used a roll of newspaper to listen to a patient's chest.

Milestones of medicine

Date	Milestone
1818	First blood transfusion
1853	First hypodermic syringe
1863	First clinical thermometer
1864	Red Cross Society formed
1865	First antiseptics used
1866	Genes first identified
1901	Blood groups (A, AB, B, O) discovered
1938	First electron microscope
1950	First kidney transplant
1956	First fibrescope used
1967	First heart transplant
1981	First heart and lung transplant

Body maps

1. Skeleton

The picture below shows the main bones in the skeleton. Most adults have 206 bones in their bodies. Very rarely, people have 11 or 13 pairs of ribs instead of the normal 12. Some also have extra vertebrae in their backs.

2. Main muscles

You have three types of muscles inside you. The muscles shown below are skeletal muscles which pull on bones. Your heart is made of cardiac muscle. The walls of your intestines and blood vessels are made of smooth muscle.

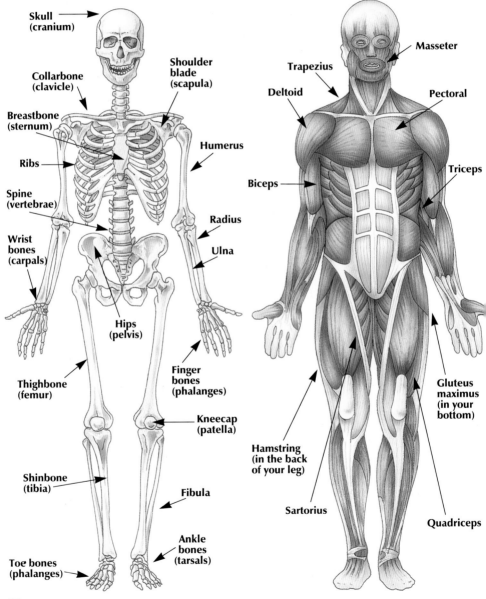

Skeleton labels:
- Skull (cranium)
- Collarbone (clavicle)
- Breastbone (sternum)
- Ribs
- Spine (vertebrae)
- Wrist bones (carpals)
- Shoulder blade (scapula)
- Humerus
- Radius
- Ulna
- Hips (pelvis)
- Thighbone (femur)
- Finger bones (phalanges)
- Kneecap (patella)
- Shinbone (tibia)
- Fibula
- Ankle bones (tarsals)
- Toe bones (phalanges)

Muscle labels:
- Masseter
- Trapezius
- Deltoid
- Pectoral
- Biceps
- Triceps
- Gluteus maximus (in your bottom)
- Hamstring (in the back of your leg)
- Sartorius
- Quadriceps

3. Main organs

Here you can see the positions of the major organs in your body. These organs work as part of your various body systems, such as your digestive, circulatory, respiratory, immune and urinary systems.

4. Communications systems

Your body has two forms of communication. Your nervous system acts on information from your senses. Your endocrine system sends chemical messengers (hormones) made in glands. Both are controlled by your brain.

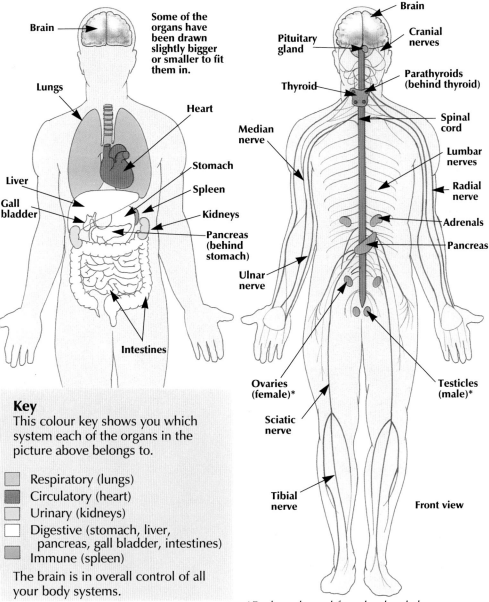

Brain

Some of the organs have been drawn slightly bigger or smaller to fit them in.

Lungs

Heart

Liver

Stomach

Spleen

Gall bladder

Kidneys

Pancreas (behind stomach)

Intestines

Brain

Pituitary gland

Cranial nerves

Thyroid

Parathyroids (behind thyroid)

Median nerve

Spinal cord

Lumbar nerves

Radial nerve

Adrenals

Pancreas

Ulnar nerve

Ovaries (female)*

Testicles (male)*

Sciatic nerve

Tibial nerve

Front view

Key

This colour key shows you which system each of the organs in the picture above belongs to.

- ☐ Respiratory (lungs)
- ☐ Circulatory (heart)
- ☐ Urinary (kidneys)
- ☐ Digestive (stomach, liver, pancreas, gall bladder, intestines)
- ☐ Immune (spleen)

The brain is in overall control of all your body systems.

*Both male and female glands have been put on one simplified diagram.

45

Glossary

Atria The two upper chambers of your heart. Also called auricles.

Blood vessels The arteries, veins and capillaries which carry blood around your body.

Cartilage Smooth, elastic, gristly tissue. One of its jobs is to cushion the ends of the two bones in a joint.

Cells The tiny units which make up all the parts of your body.

Cerebral cortex The largest part of your brain. It is divided into two halves, called hemispheres.

Chromosomes Thread-like structures in your cells, which carry your genes.

Cones Light-sensitive cells in your eyes, which detect colours.

Cranium The top part of your skull, which helps protect your brain.

Dermis The lower layer of your skin, below your epidermis.

Diaphragm The sheet of muscle under your lungs, used in breathing.

Digestion The breaking down of food into tiny particles which can be absorbed into your bloodstream.

Epidermis The upper layer of your skin, above the dermis.

Fertilization The joining of a male sperm and a female egg to make a baby.

Follicles Tiny pits, or holes, in your skin, from which hairs grow.

Genes The instructions in your cells which determine your features. They are inherited from your parents.

Germs Tiny living things which cause illnesses, called infections.

Haemoglobin The substance in your blood which makes it look red and carries oxygen around your body.

Lymph A clear fluid which travels around your body and carries white blood cells to fight infection.

Marrow A jelly-like substance inside some of your bones. It makes new red and white blood cells.

Melanin Dark pigment which gives hair, skin and eyes some of their colour.

Mucus A slimy substance which helps to protect the lining of your nose, lungs and stomach.

Neurones Another name for nerve cells.

Nutrients Substances in food which your body needs to function.

Puberty The start of the time when you change from a child into an adult.

Respiration The process by which your cells use oxygen to release energy. The waste product is carbon dioxide.

Rods Light-sensitive cells in your eyes, which detect black and white.

Sebum A natural oil made in your skin. It keeps skin supple and waterproof.

Taste buds Cells in tiny pits in your tongue, which detect flavours in food.

Ventricles The two lower chambers of your heart.

Vertebrae The separate bones which make up your spine, or backbone.

Index

First published in 1992 by Usborne Publishing Ltd, Usborne House, 83-85 Saffron Hill, London EC1N 8RT, England.
Copyright © 1992 Usborne Publishing Ltd. All rights reserved. No part of this publication may be reproduced, stored in a retrieval system, or transmitted by any means, electronic, mechanical, photocopying, recording, or otherwise, without the prior permission of the publisher.

The name Usborne and the device ♔ are Trade Marks of Usborne Publishing Ltd.   Printed in Hong Kong / China.

First published in America March 1993